MAX AN...

ADVENTURE IN ANCIENT CHINA

BY SAMANTHA METCALF

ILLUSTRATED BY IAN R. WARD

First published in Great Britain in 2017 by:
Mysteries in Time Limited
www.mysteriesintime.com

Reprinted 2021

Illustrated by Ian R. Ward
www.ianrward.co.uk

A catalogue record for this book is available from the British Library.

ISBN 978-0-9935660-9-7

Hi! I'm Katie and I am 8 years old. I think my favourite thing is playing outside in any weather. I love going to the park, especially the adventure playground with the huge, curly slide. You can go really fast on that one, especially when you lie down!

Mum hates it when I come home covered in mud, but I can't help it. The fun parts of the park are always the muddiest.

Max is my older brother. He's really clever. He helps me with my homework when I'm stuck. He knows everything! But don't tell him I said that.

My brother always looks out for me. And we have lots of fun playing games together.

Hey, I'm Max and I'm 11. I love reading. I read comics and cartoons that make me laugh, and I read adventure stories about knights and castles, or pirates and buried treasure.

I also love solving puzzles. Grandpa always buys me books full of word-searches and crosswords. I like to time myself and see how fast I can solve them.

Katie is my younger sister. She is really energetic and fun to be around, even though she can't sit still for more than five minutes! She's really fast and sporty. I wish I could be as good as her at sports. But don't tell her I said that.

I'm pleased she's my sister. We have a lot of fun together.

1

"Ouch!" shouted Max, throwing his hands up to protect his head.

Grandpa was teaching them how to fly a kite in the local park, but it wasn't going very well. It was Katie's turn to fly the kite, but the gusts of wind kept causing the kite to rise gently and elegantly, then turn and dive with force. Straight at Max's head.

"I can't help it!" shrieked Katie. "The wind keeps changing!"

"Then how come it keeps attacking ME?" said Max, ducking out of the way once again. "It never seems to land on the grass or near Grandpa - only me!"

Grandpa was watching the scene and laughing. Max was right. The kite did seem to follow Max whenever it nose-dived. It was like it was angry at him.

"Let me take over, Katie," laughed Grandpa, reaching out for the kite string. "Your mother won't be happy with me if we bring Max home covered in bruises!"

Max breathed a sigh of relief and stood up straight. He rubbed the back of his neck, where the kite had landed earlier with a crash.

"I think you should just accept that flying kites is not one of your strengths," he said to his sister.

Katie shrugged. She kicked stones all the way home.

2

Katie's mood only brightened when they turned the corner onto their street and saw the postman making his way down their street towards their house.

Max and Katie looked at each other. They didn't need to speak. They knew they were thinking the same thing: race!

They both grinned and sprinted as fast as they could. At first, Max's longer stride was winning, but it didn't take long before Katie's speed took over and she was unbeatable. They both collapsed on the grass outside their house, gasping for breath.

They had beaten the postman! He was whistling as he turned onto their garden path.

"Good morning Max and Katie," he said happily. "Who won the race?"

They were too out of breath still to talk, so Katie

waved her hand in the air.

"Then here is your prize," he said, smiling. He pulled out a large, turquoise box and presented it to Katie. It was a new adventure.

"Thank you!" she replied, jumping up and accepting the parcel like a trophy. She turned and headed inside, just as Grandpa had caught up.

"Hey, wait for me!" called Max.

Inside, Katie pulled out the Mission Plan, excited to see where this adventure would take them.

Mission Plan

Place: Ancient China
Date: 217 BC

A man called Sheng was found guilty of
stealing a dragon-shaped necklace from the
Emperor. Even though he claimed he was
innocent, he was sentenced to 10 years' hard
labour on the building site of the Great Wall.

Sadly, Sheng eventually died while working in
the harsh conditions. The jade necklace that
he was accused of stealing must have fallen
to the ground as he collapsed. It was found,
hundreds of years later, as an earthquake
caused parts of the wall to collapse.

Task:

Can you save an innocent man from this
terrible punishment? Or was Sheng guilty
after all?

3

"Ancient China!" shrieked Katie, after Max had read out the Mission Plan. "I love Chinese food, especially fortune cookies!"

Max smiled. "Actually, fortune cookies aren't really Chinese. They are believed to be a Japanese custom that was made popular in America in the 1920s."

Katie frowned. Max knew she was going to ignore that piece of information, because she liked reading the fortune inside fortune cookies.

They read all about Ancient China, learning about emperors and dynasties, as well as myths, religion and the importance of dragons.

"There were dragons in Ancient China?" asked Katie.

Max smiled. "Not real dragons," he replied. "Mythical dragons. They were believed to have magical powers and were a symbol of power and courage."

Katie groaned when she realised that kites were used in Ancient China to send messages and even to measure long distances. "Kites were originally made from silk and bamboo, before paper was invented."

"Let's hope you don't have to fly a kite on this adventure!" laughed Max.

Katie ignored him. Instead, she was excited by the clothes worn in Ancient China. "Those ladies look so pretty, with their hair tied up and decorated with flowers. And I love those long gowns! Will we get to wear something like that?"

Max nodded. "Let's get to Grandpa's shop and have a look what he has."

Katie was already out the door.

4

Max and Katie told Mum that they had to return the kite to Grandpa. They hoped that Mum didn't realise this was a lie, that Grandpa had kept the kite in his hand the whole way home.

"Alright Max," she called from the garden, where she was planting seeds and cutting flowers for a vase. "Look after your sister."

They walked the short distance to Grandpa's fancy dress shop, where they found Grandpa dancing to a song on the radio.

"Oh, er, hello young Max and Katie," he spluttered, clearly embarrassed. He turned down the radio and smoothed his hair. "I wasn't expecting you so soon! What can I do for you?"

"We, er, we are learning about Ancient China and wanted to wear some old-style clothes," explained Katie.

"Oh, yes, follow me!" said Grandpa brightly. He twirled on the spot and danced all the way to the back of the shop.

Max and Katie copied him, dancing and giggling the whole way. Once they reached the clothes rail, Grandpa twirled once again, followed by Max then Katie. Unfortunately, Katie was a little too enthusiastic and lost her balance. She landed with a thump on the ground.

Grandpa helped her up. "You have clearly inherited my dance moves," laughed Grandpa.

Katie forgot very quickly about being embarrassed, because she had spotted the brightly-coloured gowns on the rack in front of them.

They each picked a gown and Grandpa showed them how to wrap it around themselves. Max picked a red gown with black edges. His was shorter than Katie's, so he also had black trousers to wear.

Katie chose a white gown with red edges that

reached the ground. They admired themselves in the mirror. They had fun making shapes with their long, wide sleeves.

"Thanks Grandpa!" they called, as they left the shop. Grandpa didn't hear. He was already turning up the volume on the radio as they closed the door behind them.

Back home, Max and Katie raced upstairs, being careful not to trip up on their long gowns.

Katie stopped in her tracks halfway up the stairs,

causing Max to bump into her.

"What's the matter?" he asked. "Have we forgotten something?"

"I have an idea," she said.

Katie raced back down the stairs and into the kitchen. Max was confused, but he carried on upstairs to his bedroom, where he pulled out the Time Travel Sticker.

Katie came bounding back up the stairs and jumped into the room.

"Ta dah!" she sang, holding her arms out wide and turning her head to one side. She had taken one of Mum's flowers from the vase in the hallway and placed it in her hair. "What do you think?"

"Nice!" replied Max. "Now we really look the part!"

Max gave Katie the Time Travel Sticker. This time, it was designed to look like a Chinese dragon. Max knew that Katie would like the colours and the design of this one, because he did too. He was right. She beamed at him.

Max programmed the Time Machine and Katie pushed the red button to start their journey through time. Their long sleeves swirled around them as the room disappeared in a colourful whirlwind.

5

Max and Katie felt solid ground beneath their feet and looked around. There were tall, snow-capped mountains in the distance, even though the weather felt warm and the sun was shining. They were outside a beautiful building with colourful tiles, which Max guessed was the palace.

Their attention was quickly drawn towards a commotion nearby. A man was being arrested by two guards who were under the instructions of another man.

"Sheng, you are being arrested for stealing from the emperor," he boomed. "You have been sentenced to ten years' hard labour. You will join the other criminals who are building the Great Wall now."

The accused man didn't say a word. He just looked confused and allowed himself to be taken away by the guards.

Max and Katie watched as the man was taken away.

"Why didn't he say something?" asked Katie. "He just accepted his fate. But if he's innocent, why not say so?!"

Max was thinking. "You're right. It does seem strange."

6

Max and Katie decided to find out more about Sheng. They were standing on a hill overlooking a village, so they started to make their way down the hill. They asked a few people in the street if they knew a man called Sheng, but nobody did.

"He must keep himself to himself," said Max. "Nobody here knows who he is!"

Eventually, just when they were giving up hope, they asked an elderly man who was busy playing dominoes outside his small house.

"Yes, I know Sheng," replied the man. "In fact, he's our neighbour. That's his house there." He pointed to a simple but clean house next door.

"Did you know that he has been arrested?" asked Katie.

"Yes," replied the old man sadly. "News travels fast here. I hear he has stolen from the emperor."

Max nodded. "Do you think he is guilty?"

The elderly man looked around anxiously. He signalled for Max and Katie to follow him away from the street. He clearly didn't want to be overheard.

"Sheng is a very kind, generous man," he whispered. "He lives a simple life, never making any fuss and never taking any more than he needs. He is not greedy and I cannot believe these terrible accusations. He never has any dealings with the palace either, so I don't understand when this could have happened. The real thief must be one of those foreign visitors arriving along this new Silk Road."

Max and Katie were surprised by how strongly this man defended Sheng. "If he is innocent, why would he be accused?" asked Max.

The old man's frown deepened. He was watching Max and Katie carefully.

"You can trust us," promised Katie. "We want to

help Sheng by finding the real thief."

The man nodded slightly. "I don't know," he started. "But it sounds like it's got something to do with the emperor's uncle. He is usually behind anything suspicious."

"Have you ever seen the jade necklace that Sheng is accused of stealing?" asked Max.

The old man's eyes widened. "A jade necklace? Was it in the shape of a dragon?"

"Yes!" exclaimed Max. "That's the one."

The old man's hand flew to his mouth. "Oh dear, I'm afraid that the accusations might be true after all," he said sadly. "Sheng always wears a jade dragon round his neck. Perhaps he stole it a long time ago. Oh dear, this is quite a shock."

Max and Katie helped the old man sit down on a nearby rock. They looked at each other. Perhaps this mission was already solved.

Perhaps Sheng was guilty after all.

7

Max and Katie thanked the old man and left him to plan their next step. They found a quiet place to talk in the shade of a tall bamboo plant.

Max started by summarising what they knew. "Sheng is an honest man, not a thief. But he is known to have the stolen necklace in his possession."

"It doesn't make sense," said Katie. "If it's so out of character, why would he have taken the necklace?"

"Let's go and talk to Sheng," suggested Max. "I think he is the only person who can make sense of this situation."

They could see the Great Wall snaking along the top of the mountains into the distance. They knew which part was being built at the moment, by all the people who were scurrying along like ants. They set off straight away.

After about an hour of walking, they had reached

the place where the wall was being built. There were soldiers standing around watching the workers.

"Many people who worked on the wall were criminals," explained Max. "We need to be careful that the soldiers don't see us talking to Sheng."

It didn't take long before they spotted Sheng. He had a pile of stones near his feet, which he was packing into a strong mound.

Max and Katie waited until the soldiers had turned their attention to a different part of the wall, then approached Sheng.

"Hi Sheng, I'm Max and this is my sister Katie," started Max. "We're here to help you."

"You can't help me now," said Sheng. "I have been found guilty, there will be no way out for me now. I just have to accept my fate."

"That's not true!" cried Katie loudly. Her hand flew to her mouth and she looked around to see if the soldiers had heard. They hadn't. "Why don't you tell us everything that happened. We should at least try."

Sheng nodded. "It's the emperor's birthday next week. I was taking some rice as a gift. Everyone takes a gift, but rice is all I could afford to give," explained Sheng. "As I arrived at the palace, the emperor's uncle was there. He was watching all the offerings with a smile on his face. I bowed to him, then when my necklace fell forward, he spotted it and froze. I was arrested immediately."

"Could you describe the necklace to us?" asked Katie.

"I can do better than that," replied Sheng. "I can show you."

Sheng reached inside the collar of his gown and pulled out a beautiful green necklace in the shape of a dragon.

Katie was admiring the necklace, when Max shook his head.

"What? They accused you of stealing this necklace, then let you keep it?!" he exclaimed. "That makes no sense!"

Sheng nodded. "I agree. I also thought it was strange, but didn't argue. I didn't want to get beaten."

"Where did the necklace come from originally?" asked Katie.

"I didn't steal it. It has always been in my possession. I always thought it must have belonged to my parents, but I have no memory of them. I grew up an orphan."

"Did the emperor's uncle explain why you were being arrested?" asked Max.

Sheng shook his head. "He questioned me for a long time, then just announced I was guilty of theft. I think that must be when you saw me. I had already been interrogated for hours."

"What questions was he asking?" asked Max.

"They were mostly about my parents, about my childhood. I told him I don't remember my parents, but it wasn't enough!"

Max was thinking. "Perhaps your parents stole the necklace many years ago," he said gently.

"I thought that too," replied Sheng. "But why would he let me keep the necklace if it's so precious to him?"

Max had no answer.

8

Max and Katie promised Sheng they would help him, then left before they got caught by the soldiers.

"We need to split up," said Max. "I'll go to the palace and see if I can spy on the emperor's uncle."

"Good idea. I'll return to the village," added Katie. "See what I can find out from Sheng's neighbours about his lost family."

They set off in their different directions.

Max arrived at the palace and couldn't believe his luck: the emperor's uncle was pacing back and forth like a caged animal in the palace courtyard. Max ducked out of sight behind a tall building, daring to peek around the edge.

The emperor's uncle did not look happy. Max saw him muttering to himself and shaking his head angrily as a nervous soldier approached him.

Max couldn't hear everything they said to each

other, because it was in whispers. However, he heard small snippets of sentences.

"Are you sure he's at the wall?" asked the emperor's uncle.

The soldier nodded his reply.

The emperor's uncle continued, but Max couldn't hear everything. "Keep him busy... must not escape... no mistakes this time!"

Max was confused. What did he mean by 'this time'?

9

Meanwhile, Katie was just arriving at Sheng's neighbour's house. Katie knocked on their door and started by introducing herself.

"Hi, my name's Katie. I was talking to you earlier about your neighbour and I wanted to ask some more questions, if you don't mind."

The elderly man stepped forward and looked around. He was checking that nobody was watching from the street. He quickly ushered Katie inside, before locking the door behind her.

"You can't be too careful," he explained. "I'm Chau and this is my wife Zhi."

"Very pleased to meet you," said Zhi, smiling. She led Katie out to a courtyard with plants and trees bursting with blossom. "My husband told me that you were here earlier offering to help Sheng."

"Yes," said Katie. "That's right. We think he is

innocent and want to find out what's going on."

"Well, how can we help?" asked Zhi, pouring Katie a cup of green tea.

"Sheng told us he has had the necklace all his life, that he thinks it belonged to his parents. Did you know his parents?" asked Katie.

Chau shook his head sadly. "No, I'm afraid we didn't. Nobody knows what happened to them. It's a mystery."

Zhi continued where her husband left off. "It all happened in the terrible year of the Snake. So many things happened that fateful year: there was an enormous earthquake, the baby emperor died when a devastating flood covered the village, the cranes flew north for the summer and didn't return for a whole year, and the Mongols attacked. A year of great tragedy for everyone in the village."

"That was the year that Sheng's parents died. Sheng arrived in this village as an orphan. He grew up in the orphanage, but quickly became a wonderful young man."

Katie thought for a moment. "What can you tell me about the emperor's uncle?"

It looked like a dark cloud passed over Chau's expression. "He is a cold man. He does not have a kind bone in his body. You cannot trust anything he says. It is all lies."

Katie was once again shocked by his anger. "And what about the emperor himself?"

Chau continued. "Nobody really knows him very well. He is kept away from the public eye by his uncle. There is a dangerous rumour that the emperor is afraid of his uncle, that it is his uncle who is really in charge."

Zhi was nodding. "Yes, I've also heard from someone who works inside the palace that he gets very angry with his nephew, because he's not interested in being an emperor," she whispered. "He's

more interested in carving patterns out of wood.
Apparently he's very good at it."

"Thank you for your help," said Katie.

"You're very welcome," replied Zhi. "What will
you do now?"

"We need to break Sheng away from the Great
Wall so we can get to the bottom of what's going on.
I just don't know how to."

Chau smiled. "I have an idea."

10

"You will need to break Sheng out of his prison duties," said Chau. "My son can help. He looks very similar to Sheng: same height, same build, same hair. He can take Sheng's place on the Great Wall so the guards don't get suspicious. Just promise to rescue him after this is all over!"

Katie thanked Chau and Zhi for their help.

She waited, while Chau went to find his son, who really did resemble Sheng.

Katie took Chau's son to meet Max at the edge of the village as planned.

On the way to the Great Wall, Katie told Max everything she had learnt about the emperor and his uncle, how what happened to Sheng's parents was a mystery, and how Chau and Zhi still believe Sheng is innocent.

In return, Max told Katie about how the

emperor's uncle was acting suspiciously. "He's definitely up to something."

They reached the spot where Sheng was still working hard in the hot summer sun. When the soldiers weren't looking, they crept up and told him their plan.

Sheng and Chau's son swapped clothes while the soldiers weren't looking. They thanked him and promised they would be back to rescue him.

There was no time to lose.

"We need to find out why the emperor's uncle is so angry, why he is so worried about you escaping," said Max. "We need to find out what happened in the past that made him send you here like this."

Sheng frowned. "How are you going to do that? He's got what he wanted. I'm a prisoner."

Max already had a plan. "We need to get him somewhere quiet, somewhere he thinks he and you are alone," he said. "You can question him there, but we will be in the shadows, listening the whole time."

Katie was nodding. "Yes! We just need somewhere quiet, but with lots of places to hide."

"I know the perfect place," smiled Sheng. "The site of the Terracotta Army. There are thousands of statues there. Nobody is allowed in, so the emperor's uncle will feel safe there."

"And lots of statues to hide behind!" exclaimed Katie. "Great idea."

"I know how we can get past the guards too," said Sheng. "There is one place that is unprotected and the gate is weak."

They set off, feeling hopeful about their plan.

11

They soon reached the safety of Sheng's home.

"How will we lure the emperor's uncle to the meeting place?" asked Katie.

"We can write him a mysterious letter," replied Max.

Katie nudged Max. "But paper hasn't been invented yet, remember?!"

Sheng disappeared into another room for a brief moment. When he returned, he had some bamboo strips fastened together. He also had a brush and a pot of ink. They wrote a note to the emperor's uncle.

I KNOW YOUR SECRET. I KNOW WHY YOU ARRESTED SHENG. THE REAL REASON. MEET ME AMONGST THE TERRACOTTA WARRIORS AT 6 O'CLOCK. I WILL BE NEAR THE MIDDLE WARRIOR. COME ALONE.

Katie clapped her hands in delight as she watched Max making the strokes of the Chinese writing. "You're writing in Chinese!" she exclaimed. "The Time Travel Sticker really does work!"

Max and Katie briefly left Sheng to deliver the message. They passed it to a guard on the door of the palace and told him it was an urgent message that must be delivered direct to the emperor's uncle. They quickly returned to Sheng's home, making sure they weren't followed.

"Now, we wait," said Max.

That afternoon, they passed the time by playing dominoes. It didn't take long before Max and Katie were enjoying themselves.

12

However, before long it was time to go.

Max, Katie and Sheng went to the place where the Terracotta Army had been built. Sheng was right; they found the wobbly gate at the back of the enormous Terracotta Army site. They made sure the coast was clear, then squeezed through the gap.

They were standing overlooking thousands and thousands of almost identical statues, all facing the same way. Katie was excited to see there were statues of horses too.

They stepped down so they were on ground level with the statues. Max and Katie were surprised to realise the statues were life size! They were the same size as an adult, so the statues towered over Max and Katie.

On closer inspection, they realised the statues weren't identical; they were very similar, but each face had something different about it, like they were modelled on real people.

"Come on," whispered Max. "We're not here to admire the statues! We're here to help Sheng."

They started to make their way to the centre of the pit, where they had arranged to meet the emperor's uncle. They weaved in and out of figures, being careful not to make any noise, while listening out for signs that someone else was here.

The sun was starting to set, which cast long shadows across the pit. They reached the centre.

Sheng went to the meeting place, while Max and Katie each found a statue's shadow to hide in.

They waited.

Katie found the whole place eerie. It felt like the warriors could come to life any minute now and arrest them. She suddenly felt very isolated, cut off from the outside world.

"Pssst!" she whispered to Max. "There are so

many statues here, how will anyone ever find us?"

Max had been thinking the same thing, suddenly worried that there would be no time for help to reach them.

"We need a sign, some sort of signal," he said, thinking out loud.

Katie had an idea. "Wait here!" she whispered, before disappearing back the way they had just come.

It was Max's turn to feel alone. But not for long, because he heard someone nearby. The emperor's

uncle had found Sheng.

"It was you? You sent that message?" snarled the emperor's uncle. "What do you think you can gain from meeting me here, except more punishment for escaping from the Great Wall?"

"Why did you punish me?" asked Sheng. "I have done nothing to you. If I have something that belongs to you, why didn't you just take it from me? I am no threat to you."

The emperor's uncle cackled. "No threat? NO THREAT?" His expression suddenly turned serious. "You are a very real threat to this dynasty."

Max tried to make sense of what he had heard. If this was never about the dragon necklace, then what? He thought back to when he first met Sheng, when he showed them the necklace. There was something at the edge of his memory. What was it?

It's not what he had, it's who he is. He is a real threat to the dynasty.

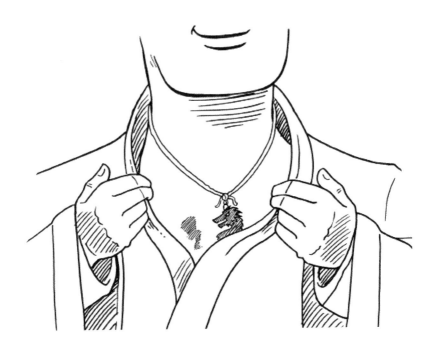

His memory flashed up an image of Sheng showing him the necklace.

That's it! He understood. He had to warn Sheng before it was too late.

Max stuck his head around the edge of the statue. The emperor's uncle had already grabbed Sheng and was tying him to the nearest statue.

"This whole area is going to be buried soon," laughed the emperor's uncle. "You will be buried with it!"

Just as Max was running out of options, Katie returned. She was out of breath, but she was carrying something. It was a kite!

"What are you going to do with that?" exclaimed Max. "Now is not exactly the time for fun."

"I saw it on the way in. It's our sign to show the soldiers where we are!" she whispered back.

Katie unravelled the string and threw the kite in the air. It fell straight back down to the ground with a thump. Katie looked around desperately.

"Where's the breeze?!" she cried.

She tried again, with the same result.

"Hurry!" hissed Max. He knew that the emperor's uncle would finish tying Sheng up soon and he must have heard the kite landing on the ground.

There was no time to lose.

Katie threw the kite in the air one last time, just as a gust of wind swirled past. The kite soared up into the sky and flew majestically above their heads.

Max was so busy watching the kite, that he didn't notice the emperor's uncle creep up, not until it was too late.

Max cried out with fear as he felt a hand grip his shoulder tightly from behind.

Katie's skills had not improved since practising with Grandpa in the park. She had no idea how to control it. She knew it was going down before she could shout out.

Max knew from experience to duck.

The emperor's uncle didn't.

The kite's nose pointed down, straight at the uncle's head. He looked up just at the moment of impact, as it hit him hard between the eyes.

Max felt the grip on his shoulder loosen as the uncle fell backwards, the kite landing on top of him.

Max high-fived his sister. "That was awesome flying, Katie!"

"Er, thanks!" she replied. It wasn't planned at all, but she didn't want to admit that now.

Max was already busy untying Sheng. Together, they used the same rope to tie the uncle up, in case he woke up soon.

The kite had not only stopped their attacker in his tracks, it had also raised the alarm. Soldiers were arriving from all directions. Max realised this looked bad: they had attacked and tied up the emperor's uncle.

They were surrounded.

13

Max, Katie and Sheng stepped closer together.

This was not looking good. Things were about to get a lot worse.

A large figure in grand robes stepped forward from the shadows. He had a long moustache that draped down either side of his chin.

It was the emperor.

He looked at each of them in turn, then his glance shifted down to his uncle tied up on the floor.

His expression was blank. It was difficult to tell what was going through his mind.

"Would somebody please explain to me what has been going on here?" he asked calmly. "Why is my uncle unconscious, tied up and apparently attacked by a kite?"

Max raised his hand to signal he wanted to speak.

"Well, er, Mr Emperor," he started. "We believe

your uncle has not been honest. About many things."

"Go on," prompted the emperor.

"This man here, Sheng, is a kind, honest and hard-working man, who keeps himself to himself," explained Max. "Then earlier today, he was arrested by your uncle for stealing from him."

"What did he steal?" asked the emperor.

"Nothing!" exclaimed Max. "It was all lies! He made Sheng think it was all about the dragon necklace that he wears around his neck, but it wasn't."

"It wasn't?!" exclaimed Sheng. "Then what exactly is it about?"

Max smiled. "You assumed it was the necklace that he had noticed when you bowed to him. But it wasn't. It was what was underneath the necklace."

"I don't understand," replied Sheng.

"You have a birthmark there that the emperor's uncle recognised.

Sheng's fingers moved to where the birthmark sat.

"What has my little birthmark got to do with the emperor's uncle?!" he asked.

"Your parents died in the terrible year of the Snake, the same year that lots of awful events took place. Events including a terrible flood, a Mongol attack, and the year the true emperor died as a baby."

Everyone was leaning in slightly towards Max, hanging on his every word.

"I think if we ask people in the palace, they will tell us that the true emperor, the baby who is said to have died that year, had a birthmark on his neck," said Max.

Katie finally understood. "So you're telling us that Sheng is the true emperor, but this evil man here on the floor pretended that he had died all those years ago, just so he could put his own nephew on the throne?"

"Yes, I think that's the truth," replied Max, nervously looking at the emperor before him. The emperor was watching Max with interest.

"Let's see if you are right," he said. He signalled for his soldiers to lift his uncle up. When he was standing upright, supported by two soldiers, the emperor spoke to him.

"Uncle, can you hear me?" he asked gently.

His uncle nodded. He was dazed from the impact of the kite.

"Did the baby emperor who tragically died in the year of the Snake have a birthmark?"

The uncle's head nodded. "Yes, on his neck! He was sent away to die, but he survived! He came back!" he replied, then took a deep breath in. "But don't worry, he cannot hurt us now. He is to be buried with the Terracotta Army. He will be no threat to your dynasty."

The emperor had heard enough.

"Take my uncle away," he ordered the soldiers. "He is sentenced to hard labour on the Great Wall, a fitting punishment, I think."

Sheng was in shock. His legs were weak, so he sat down on the ground before he collapsed. "You mean to say that all these years I didn't know the truth? That I am really the missing emperor? That cannot be true," he said, shaking his head. "I don't feel like an emperor."

The emperor bowed his head and smiled. "I know

what you mean. I still don't feel like an emperor, even after all these years," he said. "I think I always knew, deep down, that I didn't belong in the palace."

Sheng suddenly had a thought. "If I was sent away to die, then that means I'm not an orphan. Where are my parents?"

The emperor's eyes opened wide. "They are still alive!" he cried out. "They live with us in the palace. They were heart-broken when my uncle told them you had been swept away in the flood. I can't wait to tell them that you are alive."

"Did they give me the necklace?" asked Sheng.

"Yes," replied the emperor. "They believed it would keep you safe from harm. I guess they were right!"

Before Sheng followed the emperor back to the palace to meet his long-lost parents, he stopped to thank Chau and Zhi, who had joined the soldiers outside.

"You have been true friends," said Sheng. "Thank you, thank you. I will send word to the soldiers on the Great Wall to release your son."

Chau and Zhi smiled at Sheng. "We're happy that you are now safe, and that the emperor's evil uncle has been found out."

Max and Katie nodded. "Yes, and thank you for raising the alarm as we planned and calling the emperor and his soldiers," said Katie. "We couldn't have done it without you."

Max and Katie said goodbye to Sheng, who then followed the emperor back to the palace.

"Imagine meeting your parents after such a long time," said Katie. Sheng looked nervous, smoothing his hair and straightening his clothes as he walked.

"What will happen now?" asked Katie. "Do you think Sheng will become emperor?"

Max shrugged. "Perhaps. Or maybe Sheng will prefer to live the simple life and make up for lost time with his parents."

Max and Katie stepped into the shade of the nearby bamboo plants, just as the sparks of time travel started to weave around them.

They soon landed safely back in Max's bedroom. Sunshine was streaming through the window as they changed back into their normal clothes.

Katie had an idea. "Let's visit Grandpa and fly the kite again," she suggested brightly. "I think I'm really getting the hang of it now."

Max watched his sister skip down the stairs. He gulped heavily.

If only he had a hard hat to wear.

If only he had a hard hat to wear.

Also in the Mysteries in Time series:

MAX AND KATIE'S
WILD WEST ADVENTURE

WANTED
REWARD

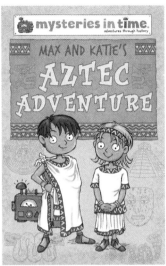

MAX AND KATIE'S
AZTEC ADVENTURE

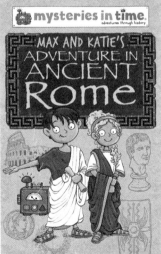

MAX AND KATIE'S
ADVENTURE IN
ANCIENT
Rome

MAX AND KATIE'S
VICTORIAN ADVENTURE